I Want to Be a Ballerina

by *Anna Membrino*

illustrated by *Smiljana Čoh*

Random House New York

I want to be a ballerina . . .

just like my sister.

I have my tights,

my leotard,

my ballet shoes,

and my TUTU!

I'm a ballerina!

"But, Mia," says my sister, "a ballerina needs balance. You tripped going up the stairs yesterday."

Wait, I just need to practice a little.

TA-DA! Now am I a ballerina?

"Not yet, Mia," says my sister.
"A ballerina needs coordination.
You knock your juice over
every morning."

Hold on, I just need to practice a little.

TA-DA! Now am I a ballerina?

"Not yet, Mia," says my sister.
"A ballerina is delicate. You clomp
around and scare the cats."

Okay, I just need to practice a little.

TA-DA!

There's more?!

"Do you want to come to ballet class with me?"

I DO!

"Come on, Mia. You're ready!"

"I'll meet you after class!"

Boy, that was hard!

"Well, it *was* your very first class."

"And, you know, Mia . . ."

"Now we can practice together!"

For Mom, Dad, and Michael.
With special thanks to Maria and John.
—A.M.

This book is dedicated to Nora, my niece!
—S.Č.

Text copyright © 2014 by Anna Membrino
Cover art and interior illustrations copyright © 2014 by Smiljana Čoh
All rights reserved. Published in the United States by Random House Children's Books,
a division of Random House LLC, a Penguin Random House Company, New York.
Random House and the colophon are registered trademarks of Random House LLC.
Visit us on the Web! randomhouse.com/kids
Educators and librarians, for a variety of teaching tools, visit us at RHTeachersLibrarians.com
Library of Congress Cataloging-in-Publication Data
Membrino, Anna.
I want to be a ballerina / by Anna Membrino ; illustrated by Smiljana Coh. — First edition.
pages cm.
Summary: Mia's big sister teaches her that there is more to being a ballerina than just putting on the right clothes.
ISBN 978-0-385-37864-2 (trade) — ISBN 978-0-375-97330-7 (lib. bdg.) — ISBN 978-0-375-98233-0 (ebook)
[1. Ballet dancing—Fiction. 2. Sisters—Fiction.] I. Coh, Smiljana, illustrator. II. Title.
PZ7.M5176Iag 2014 [E]—dc23 2013018813
Book design by John Sazaklis
MANUFACTURED IN CHINA
10 9 8 7 6 5 4 3
First Edition
Random House Children's Books supports the First Amendment and celebrates the right to read.